ORCHARD BOOKS

First published in Great Britain in 2016
by The Watts Publishing Group
This edition first published in 2017

13

Text © Rachel Bright, 2016
Illustrations © Jim Field, 2016

A CIP catalogue record for this book is
available from the British Library.

ISBN 978 1 40833 164 4

Printed and bound in Italy

MIX
Paper from
responsible sources
FSC® C015829
FSC
www.fsc.org

Orchard Books
An imprint of Hachette Children's Group
Part of The Watts Publishing Group Limited
Carmelite House, 50 Victoria Embankment,
London EC4Y 0DZ

An Hachette UK Company
www.hachette.co.uk

www.hachettechildrens.co.uk

For my wonderful,
brilliant, adventureful
dad . . . the most CAN-DO
Kevin I know x — R B

For Remi and Jack — J F

THE KOALA WHO COULD

Rachel Bright   Jim Field

ORCHARD

In a wonderful place,
at the breaking of dawn,
Where the breezes were soft
and the sunshine was warm,

A place where the creatures
ran wild and played free . . .
A koala called Kevin
clung to a tree.

A nicer grey fellow
you never would meet,
As SOFT as a SOFT THING
from ear-tufts to feet.

His favourite way
to relax in the sun,
Was to cling and to nap
and to munch a leaf-bun.

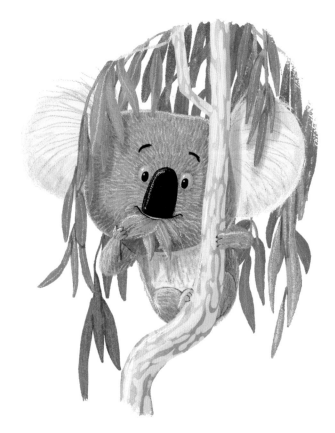

He was terribly good
at all these three things —

Yes, Kevin was KING
of the STAYING-STILL KINGS.

You see, high up was safe since he liked a slow pace,

While the ground down below seemed a frightening place.

TOO FAST

and TOO LOUD

and TOO BIG

and TOO STRANGE.

Nope. Kevin preferred not to move, nor to change.

So he clung to his tree

as he knew how to do,

And was never too keen

to try anything new.

So when Wombat stopped by,

and shouted one day,

"HEY, KEVIN! Why don't you

come down here and play?"

"Um . . . I think," he replied,
"I should stay on my plant.
I'm busy right now . . .
No. I'm sorry. I can't."

"WHY NOT?" cried the roos,
who liked the idea.
"YES, WHY?" called the dingos.
"YOU'VE NOTHING TO FEAR!"

But Kevin, who wasn't
the 'do-things-quick' sort,
Said, "I've clinging to do.
But thanks for the thought."

As Kevin sat watching

them chatter and share,

A part of him wished

he could join in down there.

But he knew he'd miss home
in the dark and the late.

The whole thing was risky,
adventure could wait.

Whatever the invite,
he'd always say **NO**.
Oh dear, it seemed Kevin . . .

. . . just couldn't let go.

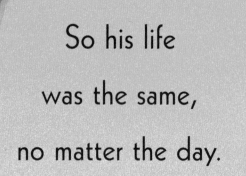

So his life
was the same,
no matter the day.

The weeks
came and went, and the
months rolled away.

And Kevin stayed still
while the world
moved around,

Until he
awoke to a
WORRYING sound . . .

TAP TAP TAP TAP

TAP TAPPITY TAP

The sound went

Well . . . this was a blow!

"**UN-CLING!**"
the crowd called,
that had gathered below.

"Leap and we'll
catch you!
Just let yourself go!"

But Kevin was scared.

"Let go?
NO, I shan't!"

"I won't!"
clung on Kevin.
"Oh dear, I JUST...

WHOOOOOOMPF!

Down came the tree
with a cracking and pinging.
Crash and a **WALLOP**. . .
with Kevin still clinging!

Kevin, he carefully opened one eye

and looked up at the love staring down from the sky.

Then one-claw by one-claw, he slowly un-clung . . .

He felt SPRINGY and

LIGHT and

HAPPY and

YOUNG!

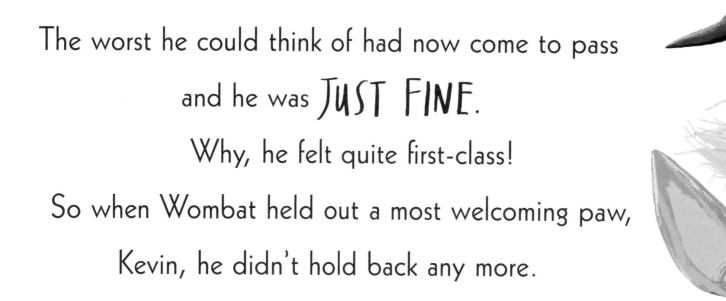

The worst he could think of had now come to pass
and he was JUST FINE.
Why, he felt quite first-class!
So when Wombat held out a most welcoming paw,
Kevin, he didn't hold back any more.

When Dingo asked, "Now will you come out to play?"

The crowd all joined in with a "what-do-you-say?"

And even though this wasn't part of his plan,

Kevin replied, "Yes! I think that . . .

I CAN"

And Kevin, from then on,
was always CAN-DO...

Because life can be GREAT
when you try something NEW!